Stars Above Us

By **Geoffrey Norman**

Illustrated by **E. B. Lewis**

G. P. Putnam's Sons ✶ **Penguin Young Readers Group**

G. P. PUTNAM'S SONS

A division of Penguin Young Readers Group.

Published by The Penguin Group. Penguin Group (USA) Inc., 375 Hudson Street, New York, NY 10014, U.S.A. Penguin Group (Canada), 90 Eglinton Avenue East, Suite 700, Toronto, Ontario M4P 2Y3, Canada (a division of Pearson Penguin Canada Inc.). Penguin Books Ltd, 80 Strand, London WC2R 0RL, England. Penguin Ireland, 25 St. Stephen's Green, Dublin 2, Ireland (a division of Penguin Books Ltd.). Penguin Group (Australia), 250 Camberwell Road, Camberwell, Victoria 3124, Australia (a division of Pearson Australia Group Pty Ltd). Penguin Books India Pvt Ltd, 11 Community Centre, Panchsheel Park, New Delhi - 110 017, India. Penguin Group (NZ), 67 Apollo Drive, Rosedale, North Shore 0632, New Zealand (a division of Pearson New Zealand Ltd.). Penguin Books (South Africa) (Pty) Ltd, 24 Sturdee Avenue, Rosebank, Johannesburg 2196, South Africa. Penguin Books Ltd, Registered Offices: 80 Strand, London WC2R 0RL, England.

Manufactured in China by South China Printing Co. Ltd.

Design by Richard Amari.

Text set in Garamond.

Library of Congress Cataloging-in-Publication Data

Norman, Geoffrey. Stars above us / Geoffrey Norman ; illustrated by E.B. Lewis. p. cm. Summary: A little girl's father helps her get over her fear of the dark before he goes off to war, and she uses the stars they painted on her ceiling to remind her of him while he is away. [1. Fear of the dark—Fiction. 2. Separation (Psychology)—Fiction. 3. Stars—Fiction. 4. Fathers and daughters—Fiction. 5. Children of military personnel—Fiction.] I. Lewis, Earl B., ill. II. Title. PZ7.N7842St 2009 [E]—dc22 2008027731

ISBN 978-0-399-24724-8

10 9 8 7 6 5 4 3 2 1

*A*manda's father had read her a story. He had tucked her in and given her a kiss. He was about to turn out the light when Amanda said, "I don't want to go to sleep."

"Why not?" Daddy asked.

"I'm afraid of the dark."

Daddy reached down and hugged her, and then picked her up in his arms. He felt big and strong.

"The dark?" Daddy said. "That's nothing to be afraid of."

"But scary things live in the dark."

"No. Wonderful, fun things live in the dark. Let's go look for some."

When they were outside, Daddy said, "Look all around you and tell me what you see."

"Fireflies!" said Amanda.

There were a lot of them, blinking in the air like tiny lanterns. Off and on. Glowing yellow spots in the dark.

"Are they scary?"

"No," Amanda said. "They're not scary. They're *fun*."

Then Daddy pointed to some stars and told her they were called the Big Dipper, and he showed her how they pointed to another star, one that looked especially big and bright. "That's the North Star, and it is always in the same place in the sky," her dad said. "It's a special star."

Amanda looked all around the sky at all of the stars. So many of them, and some of them were twinkling. Like the fireflies.

"Stars are beautiful," said Amanda.

Amanda and Daddy watched the fireflies and the stars, and listened to the crickets.

"Are the crickets scary?" asked Daddy.

"No. They sound nice."

"It's night music."

And then it was time to go back inside.

"But my room is still dark and scary," Amanda said. "It doesn't have stars and fireflies."

"We'll fix that," Daddy told her.

The next day, Daddy came home carrying a bag. He said it was "A bag full of stars. Beautiful stars for Amanda."

"That's just paper and paste and paint and stuff. There aren't any stars in there," Amanda said when she looked in the bag.

"Not yet," Daddy said.

Amanda and her mom and dad drew stars on the paper and cut them out.

Soon, there were lots of paper stars in the middle of the table.

"Now, let's paint them with this," Daddy said.

It was special paint that would glow in the dark, he explained.

"Then, we will paste them on your ceiling," said Daddy.

Amanda couldn't wait for it to get dark.

At bedtime, Daddy turned off the light and said, "What do you think?"

Amanda looked at the ceiling and said, "It's just like being outside and looking up into the sky."

"And is it scary?"

"No. It isn't. I love it!"

"See that star?" Daddy said, and pointed to the biggest one. "That's the North Star. Like the one we saw together, outside. You can see it from anywhere in the world. When I am away, you can look at it and think of me. It will be our star."

"Will you be gone a long time?" Amanda asked.

"Yes. When I get home, you will be so much bigger, and you can tell me about everything that happened while I was away."

Amanda hugged her dad. She already missed him.

On the last day before he went away, Amanda's daddy said, "I have another surprise for you."

"What is it?"

"Close your eyes."

Amanda did, and when she opened them, her daddy was holding a puppy.

"I love him!" Amanda said. "What's his name?"

"I thought we'd call him Bear. That's another name for the Big Dipper, the stars I showed you."

Every night after her daddy
went away, Amanda would look
at the Big Dipper and the North
Star and think of him.

"That's *our* star, Bear," she
would say. "Yours, mine, and
Daddy's."

"Amanda," her mother said one day. "Guess who's calling?"

When Amanda picked up the phone, her dad said, "How's my girl?"

She was so excited, she almost couldn't talk.

"Are you coming home today?" Amanda said.

"Not today," Daddy said. "Soon, though. And you know what?"

"What?"

"It's night where I am, on the other side of the world. And I'm looking up at our star and thinking about you."

"I want you to come home," Amanda said.

"I will, soon," said Daddy. "And I want you to do something for me."

"What?"

"When you go to bed tonight, look up at our star and make a wish. Make a wish for me to come home soon."

"I will."

Amanda and her mom sat on the bed. They sat
very close so Amanda could comb her mother's hair.
"Are you scared for Daddy?" Amanda said.
"Yes, sweetie," Mommy said. "He's so far away."
"Is it dangerous where he is?"
"Yes, it is. Your dad is a brave man."

One day, when they were on a walk with Bear, Amanda's mom said, "Daddy is going to be so surprised when he sees how big Bear has gotten. And you, too."

"I know," Amanda said. "And I want to have another surprise ready for him."

"What kind of surprise?"

Amanda told her.

"That's wonderful," Mommy said. "I'll help you."

The day finally came. Amanda and her mother drove to the airport to meet her dad. She was so happy when she saw him with the other soldiers. Daddy hugged them both and then he picked Amanda up and said, "See? You must have wished on our star, because here I am. Home."

"I did wish," Amanda said. "Every night. And guess what?"

"What?"

"I have a surprise for you when we get home."

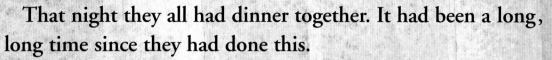

That night they all had dinner together. It had been a long, long time since they had done this.

"I'm so glad to be home," Daddy said. "But where is my surprise?"

"I'll show you," Amanda said, "but first you have to close your eyes."

When her dad had closed his eyes, Amanda held his hand and led the way upstairs and into her room. She turned out the lights, then said, "Okay, now open your eyes."

Her dad opened his eyes and saw that there were more stars on the ceiling. And a moon. And comets, too. Amanda and her mom had made them. And they had made fireflies, too, out of yarn they painted with the special paint. They hung them from the ceiling with pieces of thread. The room was full of glowing, happy things, just like outside.

"It's beautiful," Daddy said. "What a great surprise."

Later that night, Amanda woke up. It was still dark.
The crickets were still singing and the stars and the moon
and the comets glowed on the ceiling. She looked at
them, and then out at the real sky and at the special star.

"Thank you," she said to the North Star. Then she
went back to sleep. Her dad was home.